For Frank K. Major (Kyle)
Thank you for all you've done, including being the proudest supporter of Dee Write and the Little Ruth Series as well as being the most amazing dad to our four "Little Ruths."

Little Ruth First Day of School
Text Copyright © 2023 Little Ruth LLC
Illustrations Copyright © 2023 Little Ruth LLC

All rights reserved. No part of this publication may be reproduced, distributed, or transmitted in any form or by any means, including photocopying, recording, or other electronic or mechanical methods, without the prior written permission of the publisher, except in the case of brief quotations embodied in critical reviews and certain other noncommercial uses permitted by copyright law. For permission requests, write to info@littleruth.com. Write "Attention: Permissions" in the subject line.

www.LittleRuth.com

ISBN 979-8-35091-705-5

First Edition

First Day of School

Written by Dee Write

Illustrated by Andrea McAllister

Summer break had come to an end, and it was almost the first day of school. Ruth and her siblings—Timmy, Annie, and Abby—were all starting at a new school. Ruth and Timmy were feeling excited and a little nervous.

"Ruth, are you ready to go to our new school?" Timmy asked. "'Cause I'm a little scared."

"I know. I'm kinda scared too, but I'm also happy to make some new friends! I think if we're nice, other kids will be nice to us too!"

Annie and Abby groaned at the mention of bedtime. "Awww, but Daaaddeee, we don't wanna go to bed!"

"I know," said Dad, "but I promise to read you one more story before you go to sleep!"

"Okay!" The twins exclaimed in unison.

That night, Mom helped Ruth lay out her clothes, and Ruth added her special charms to her favorite bracelet. She also added charms to her new book bag, and she packed her school supplies. Ruth was feeling nervous about school, but adding these special touches gave her some extra sparkle and reminded her to have courage.

After Dad tucked her in, Ruth fell asleep thinking about the fun and fright of starting a new school and making new friends. It would be a big adventure, but Ruth knew that being nice to everyone and trying her best would help her feel confident.

The next day when they arrived at the new school, it was bigger and busier than they remembered from their visit.

"Wow!" Ruth exclaimed. "Look at that big slide on the playground!"

"Yeah!" agreed Timmy. "I can't wait to play on it!"

At the beginning of class, Ruth and her classmates participated in an icebreaker, and Ruth told everyone all about herself.

"Hi, I'm Ruth! I like art, and I love to decorate things, like my clothes. Sometimes, I even decorate my book bag or make bracelets!"

After the icebreaker, the teacher, Miss Flowers, told the kids about after-school clubs. Miss Flowers gave the students a list of clubs to take home and read with their parents. Ruth saw lots of clubs that interested her, but the arts and crafts club excited her the most.

Soon, it was lunchtime, and it was Ruth's first chance to connect with new friends. Ruth grabbed her lunch and looked around for a place to sit, but it seemed like everyone was already sitting with friends. Even though Ruth had worn her special charm bracelet and was friendly to everyone, she still felt too shy to walk up to new groups of kids.

Just as Ruth began to feel uneasy and queasy about her lunchtime dilemma, she saw Timmy sitting with some friends.

Ruth had not planned to sit with her younger brother and his friends, but it was better than sitting alone. Ruth walked over to the table with Timmy and sat down. She tried to be interested in his friends' conversation about action figures, but she felt sad that she didn't sit with any of her own classmates.

By the time Mom picked up the kids at school, Ruth no longer felt her best. In the car, Mom asked everyone about their day. Everyone excitedly shared, but Ruth stayed mostly quiet.

Once they were home, Mom asked everyone to clean out their book bags and give her any papers from school. Ruth was cleaning out her bag when Mom stood next to her.

"Ruth, you haven't said very much since school pickup. Is everything okay?" Mom asked.

"I feel a bit sad," Ruth answered. At lunch I did not have anyone to sit with, so I sat with Timmy and his friends. It was nice of Timmy and his friends to let me sit with them, but I wished I had my own friends to sit with."

"Aw, Ruth. I'm sorry that happened, and I understand why it makes you feel sad," Mom said. What do you think we can do to make tomorrow feel better?"

Ruth handed Mom the after-school clubs list. "I wanted to join the arts and crafts club, but now I'm not so sure."

Mom encouraged Ruth. "Sometimes we feel unsure about ourselves after things do not go as we hoped. When this happens to me, I list ways to try to make it better. Would you like to list a few things for you to try tomorrow?"

"Okay," Ruth agreed.

Ruth and Mom came up with three ideas for Ruth to try.

⭐ Join the arts and crafts club.

⭐ Play with one or more new friends during morning recess.

⭐ Ask to sit with new friends during lunch.

Ruth agreed to try at least one idea, and maybe she would try two ideas or all three. Best of all, having a plan helped her feel like her sparkle was coming back.

The next day at school, when Ruth thought about her plan, her tummy felt topsy-turvy. But Ruth knew she had to try her best. During morning recess, Ruth saw a classmate, Rose, climbing the rock wall. Ruth asked Rose if they could climb together, and Rose agreed.

When they finished climbing, Ruth and Rose joined some classmates in a game of kickball. By the time recess was over, Ruth had made two new friends, Rose and Sofia.

At lunch, Ruth saw Rose and Sofia sitting. "Can I sit with you?" Ruth asked quietly. Rose and Sofia were happy to have Ruth join them. The girls talked about school and their favorite lunch foods.

During afternoon recess, Ruth joined a different group of classmates on the jungle gym. She saw a boy standing by himself, and she invited him to play. His name was Chris, and he was happy to play with a new friend.

Ruth's plan was working great, and she even got to help others. This made Ruth feel good, and she was proud of herself for trying.

After school, Ruth went to her arts and crafts club. The club teacher, Miss Patsy, had set up choice time stations. Kids from other classes that Ruth did not know were already settled into their activities.

Ruth took a deep breath and sat next to a girl she didn't know but who was making bracelets and necklaces, just like Ruth liked to do.

After a few minutes, Ruth said, "I really like your bracelet. Can I use some of the same pink beads?"

"Sure!" she said. "I'm Charlotte!"

"I'm Ruth," Ruth said. The girls talked and played for the rest of club time. Ruth learned that Charlotte and she were in the same grade, and Charlotte had little sisters, just like Ruth.

Soon the bell rang, and it was time to go home. Ruth waved goodbye to Charlotte as she climbed in the car with Mom.

"Well, how did it go today, Ruth?" asked Mom, seeing how happy Ruth looked.

"It was the best day ever!" Ruth exclaimed. Ruth and Mom gave each other a high-five.

"Yesss! I knew you could do it!" said Mom, and the two talked excitedly about Ruth's day on the way home.

Ruth had all her sparkle back, and she felt like her best self again. This was going to be a great school year!

The End

Featured Adinkra Symbols

ONYANKOPON ADOM NTIBIRIBIARA BEYE VIE represents hope, providence, and faith and translates to "by God's grace, all will be well." The symbol's image looks like a protected heart.

TABONO represents unity of purpose, strength, confidence, and hard work to reach your goal. Tabono translates to "oar" or "paddle," and the symbol looks like four oars paddling toward a destination.

We chose these symbols for *First Day of School* because they remind us that sometimes, you just have to have the heart to move forward in providence, with hope and strength, and having faith and confidence that all will be well (even when it's difficult). Ruth demonstrates positivity, hope, confidence, and a lot of heart and bravery when she goes to school and tries new ways to make friends! Way to go, Ruth!

For more on Dee Write's use of these Adinkra symbols in *First Day of School*, visit this QR Code.